VOICES
IN FIRST PERSON

VOICES

REFLECTIONS ON LATINO IDENTITY

EDITED BY LORI MARIE CARLSON

PHOTOGRAPHS BY MANUEL RIVERA-ORTIZ

ILLUSTRATIONS BY FLAVIO MORAIS

ATHENEUM BOOKS FOR YOUNG READERS
NEW YORK LONDON TORONTO SYDNEY

IN FIRST PERSON

Atheneum Books for Young Readers

An imprint of Simon & Schuster

Children's Publishing Division

1230 Avenue of the Americas,

New York, New York 10020

Book design by Debra Sfetsios

The text for this book is set in Bell MT.

Manufactured in the United States of America

First Edition

10 9 8 7 6 5 4 3 2 1

Library of Congress Cataloging-in-Publication Data

Voices in first person: reflections on Latino identity /

edited by Lori Marie Carlson. — 1st ed.

p. cm.

Summary: A collection of brief fictional pieces

about the experiences of Latinos in the

United States, by such writers as Sandra Cisneros,

Gary Soto, Oscar Hijuelos, and others.

ISBN-13: 978-1-4169-0635-3

ISBN-10: 1-4169-0635-5

1. Hispanic Americans—Literary collections.

[1. Hispanic Americans—Literary collections.]

I. Carlson, Lori M.

PZ5.V76 2008

[Fic]—dc22

2008053161

For my young friend Azula Carmen Wilson,
and in memory of William Sloane Coffin, Jr.,
prophet, leader, teacher
—L.M.C.

acknowledgments

I wish to acknowledge the following individuals
who, in 2005 and 2006, as I was finishing this book,
helped to sustain me through much loss. First my
husband, Oscar, and my parents, Robert and Marie;
sister Leigh Ann and brother-in-law Larry; my
agent, Jennifer Lyons; my editor, Caitlyn Dlouhy;
and last, but certainly not least, champions Karen
Levinson, Allen Brill, and Ashley Normand. In my
midst, too, were caring friends and neighbors: Carol
and Jeffrey, Lou and Laurie, Jenny and Jamie, Roger,
Meg and Mark, David and Sue, Jonathan, Monroe,
Edith, Shirley, Beatriz, Carmen, Barbara and Jim,
and Marilyn. And farther afield, in other states and
countries, were friends whose prayers and kindness
reminded me to look for beauty: Marjorie and John,
Ylva, Constanza, and Pina. Thank you all.
For your humanity.

a note on the texts

Some of the monologues in this collection ignore
correct spelling and diacritical usage. Rather than
altering such instances—so as to make these
particular monologues conform to standard written
English and Spanish—I have chosen to respect the
authors' artistic license and creative grammar
and punctuation. It is my wish to emphasize the
liveliness and whimsy of the spoken word so that
the underlying rhythm and freedom of the authors'
syntax comes through loud and clear.

CONTENTS

EDITOR'S

NOTE

by Lori Marie Carlson

THE TEENAGE YEARS ARE YEARS OF EMOTION, ALL KINDS OF EMOTION.

LOVE, HATE, BETRAYAL, HILARITY, LOSS,

LONGING, FEELING MAD, FEELING SAD . . .

these are but some of the emotional states given voice by

accomplished Latino authors—among them Esmeralda

Santiago, Melinda Lopez, Trinidad Sánchez Jr., Oscar

Hijuelos, Sandra Cisneros, and Quiara Alegría Hudes—in

this book. In a sense *Voices in First Person* is a collection of monologues that can be read aloud in the classroom—in theater workshops, social studies, English language labs, ESL, literature courses—or in the privacy of your room, at a community center, in a field of flowers, in the basement of a church, or on the street. But I think this collection of narratives, some short and others long, can also be considered a multitestimonial of lives in inner cities, rural communities, suburbs, and villages. These pieces speak truths—sometimes hard truths—about the incredibly diverse life experiences of youth in America today, Latino or otherwise. With their sometimes biting potency and bouncing lyricism, they are earthy and powerful. They grab at the heart and the mind because they say it like it is. And there is something here for everyone. These fictional narratives are proclamations of pride, cries of despair, funny reflections on food and family, angry shouts, fearful thoughts of giving birth, revelations about God, whispers of hopelessness, declarations of violence, admissions of passion, love, and hope.

A GIRL IMAGINES

by Claudia Quiroz Cahill

THE HOMELAND OF HER MOTHER.

RITUAL

Mami, come sit down. The day is over. Let's smile a bit. Do you think you'll have that flying dream again? The one where you open all the glittering windows, float out above the rose-painted *casitas*, the opaque trees, the soft llama grass, to Bolivia, back to your home, before I was born. I can only imagine the sound of flutes, the sound of women singing. Ancient song. Andean *villancicos.* A metronome ticks in my chest. Bolivia, Bolivia, the Spanish sounds, Bolivia, my tongue snails over, Bolivia, Bolivia, making my teeth clean. In a room full of notes I rise up, good as new.

1

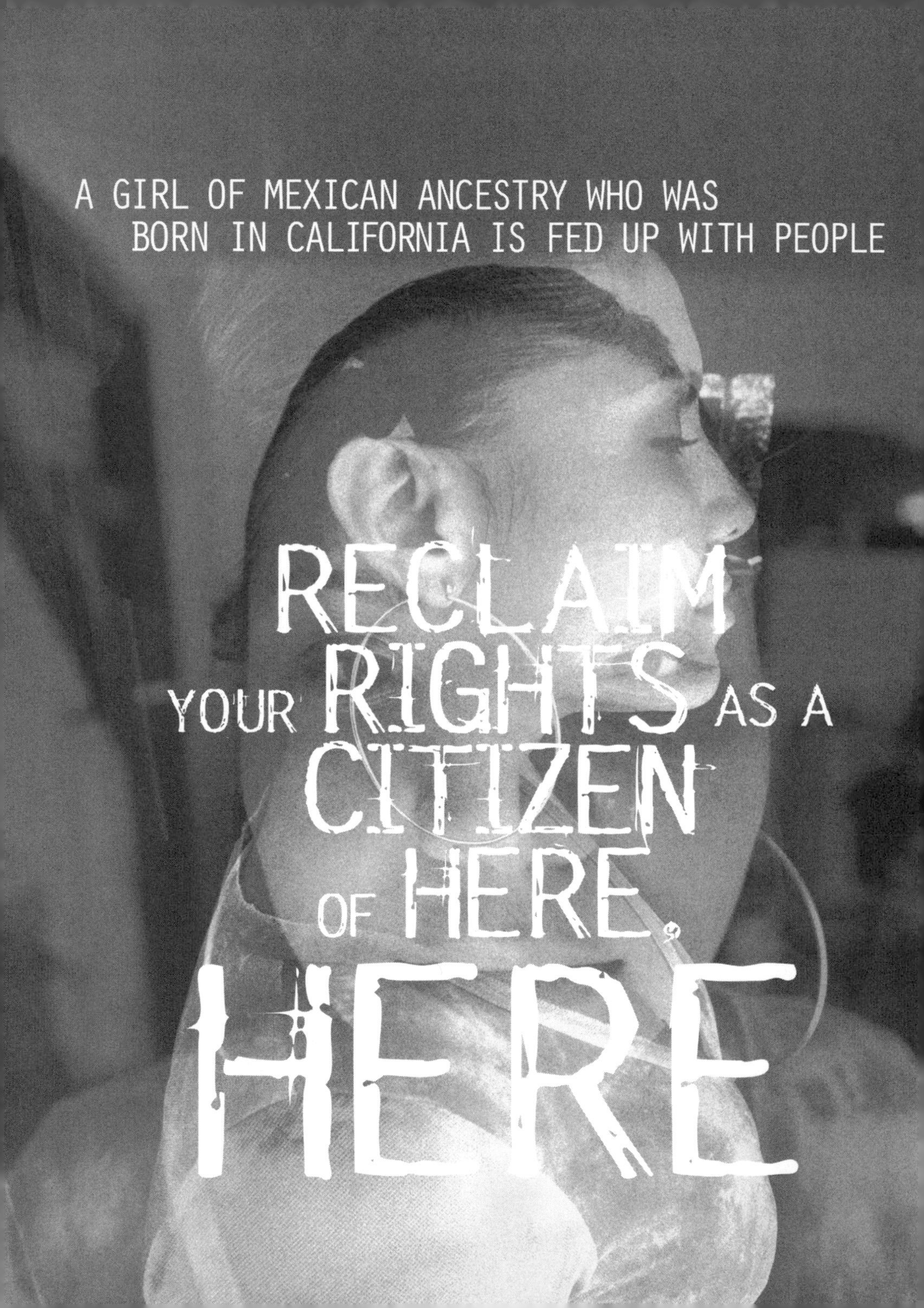

A GIRL OF MEXICAN ANCESTRY WHO WAS
BORN IN CALIFORNIA IS FED UP WITH PEOPLE

RECLAIM
YOUR RIGHTS AS A
CITIZEN
OF HERE,
HERE

by Michele Serros

ASKING HER WHERE SHE IS FROM.

I can't get by one week without a white person asking me
the Question:

> "So, where are you from?"
> "From Oxnard," I answer.
> "No, I mean originally."
> "Oh, Saint John's Hospital,
> the old one over on F Street."
> "No, you know what I mean!"

No, what do you mean? And why is it important to
you and why do you really need to know? When Latinos
ask me where I'm from, it really doesn't bother me. I can't
help but feel some sort of familiar foundation is being
sought and a sense of community kinship is forming.
"Your family's from Cuernavaca? And what? They own
the IHOP on Via San Robles? Wow, we really need to do
lunch sometime!"

But when whites ask me the Question, it's just a
reminder that I'm not like them, I don't look like them,
which must mean I'm not from here. Here in California,
where I was born, where my parents were born, and
where even my great-grandmothers were born. I can't

help but feel that whites always gotta know the answer to everything. It's like they're uncomfortable not being able to categorize things they're unfamiliar with, and so they need to label everything as quickly and neatly as possible. Sometimes when I'm asked the Question, I like to lie and make up areas within the Latin world from where I supposedly originated:

> WHITE PERSON #1. **So, where did you say you're from?**
> ME. **From Enchiritova, it's actually a semipopulated islet off the coast of Bolivia.**
> WHITE PERSON #2. **Yep! I knew it! I knew it! Kevin, didn't I tell you I thought she was an Enchirito!**
> WHITE PERSON #1. **Tag her!**

by Gary Soto

A BOY, AGE FOURTEEN, IS HOLDING

Ben Franklin said something like "A penny saved is a penny earned." I think a lot of people lived by this rule. Let me go back three days. . . . Uncle Joe was waking up on his couch, poor old Uncle with more hair in his ears than on his head. I walked up the steps, looked in the window of his little house, and I caught him sleeping, two sweaters on 'cause he's so cheap the thought of body heat escaping makes him shiver. I called, "Uncle," and he rose straight like a corpse in a coffin, spooky like. He rubbed his eyes, looked at me, and said, "You were supposed to be here this morning!" You see, my mom and my aunts had told me if I was a really good boy, I should do volunteer work—work for the family, is what they meant. (*Pause.*) So Uncle let me in the house, real quick because he didn't want the furnace heat to escape—he was tight there, too. He let me in the house to get to the backyard—no gates on the side of his house 'cause that cost money. But first, in the kitchen, he swallowed three prunes like goldfish and said, "You can have one if you want." He thrust a nasty-looking jar at me, and I said, "Nah, Unc, I had my Cap'n Crunch this morning. I'm here to work." (*Pause.*) So then out in the yard he was asking if he had ever told me the story 'bout how the tips of his boots got run over by a German tank

SPENDING MONEY

A RAKE.

in World War II. I told him, "Yeah, lots of times, and the one about making a broom out of twigs in 1932." All mad, he turned his dentures upside down like fangs. He said, "I don't know how your teeth stay in your face, always talking that way. Do you talk like that with your friends?" I almost said, "Yeah,

A FEW LEAVES ARE

SCATTERED AROUND HIM.

about the same as you talking 'bout the war." Then those
prunes made him fart, and I jumped away and got to work
stirring up the leaves for some air sweeter than the wind
he just released. He went away, and I raked the yard clean,
then poked an orange down from the tree. Uncle came
out happy and stood on the back porch. He had put on yet
another sweater and righted his dentures so his fangs were
gone. "Pretty days don't cost nothing," old Stingy quipped.
I twirled the rake and muttered, "That's why you never
had a girlfriend. They cost money." He made his bushy
eyebrows go up and down, and said, "I didn't hear what you
said, but I know it was something smart-alecky." He told
me that he was in such a good mood that nothing was
going to make him mad, especially a snotty teenager like
me. He then started telling me stuff like when to plant
tomato seeds, and I made a thousand faces to show how
interested I was. He gave me three quarters for my work,
and I said, "Gee, Unc, I just might go buy me some
tomato seeds." "What?" he asked, and I answered,
"Nothing, Unc." Then, with one hand on the rail, he
climbed down the porch steps, farting every other one.
I backed away and crumpled a leaf in my hand for some
neutralizing odor. He gave me a look and said, "Nephew,
how far do you think you'll go from the money I've given

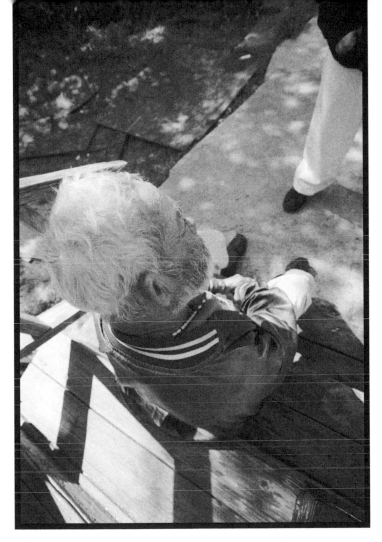

you over the years?" I looked around the yard, with a smirk
playing on my face, and I said, "Maybe to that rosebush
there, or far as the orange tree." With that, Uncle turned
his dentures upside down again like fangs. He twisted open
my palm and rolled those quarters back into the leathery
pouch of his tightfisted hand. (*Pause.*) I don't know who's
older, Ben Franklin or my uncle in three sweaters.

I STAND
AT THE CROSSWALK

I stand at the crosswalk on Main Street. The speed limit is twenty-five miles per hour, so drivers must slow down through the three blocks that compose the center of this small town, its storefronts featuring balsam pillows, pure maple syrup, real beeswax candles, hormone-free cheddar cheese. When they notice me, most drivers do a double take. In the summer there are many tourists in this charming town, and some of them are as dark as, or even darker than, I am. But by late fall they have gone away with their "Made in Vermont" products and digital pictures of foliage at its colorful peak. I am here in the off-season. The locals who peer in my direction seem to be asking, *Who are you and what are you doing here?* Maybe I'm sensitive. Maybe they're questioning not my dark skin and dreadlocks, but rather my presence where tourists are rare this time of year. Maybe I'm reading too much into their looks. Maybe years of noticing such looks have caused me to automatically interpret them with much more malice than is

by Esmeralda Santiago

A GIRL IS WATCHING PEOPLE WATCHING HER.

intended. I don't know. I don't know whether it's me
or them, but it bothers me. It bothers me a lot, but
I don't know what to do about it except to let them
stare. If we make eye contact, I smile. Sometimes
they smile back. Most often, however, they return
their gaze to the road and keep driving, pretending,
maybe hoping, that they didn't see me.

by Gwylym Cano

(Prison. Pale morning light falls on Angel, a Chicano. Short. Tough. Mean. Tattoos. Inmate uniform. Doors open and close. Guards shout. In the distance, men, conversations.)

ANGEL'S MONOLOGUE

Doors close. Open. People come, go. Nobody leaves unless you leave for good. *Órale.* There aren't words to describe it. This is how it is—state, Califas. Country of origin, Aztlan. Who am I—do you care? Bullet. Name's Bullet, and I'm comin' right at you. *Blam.* Nah. I'm not the fuzz. I've had other names. I've been other people. Bullet had a baby named Gun. *(Points finger at his own head.)* *Blam. Blamblam.* That's funny. See, in my fantasy I live long enough to shoot myself two more times. That's how you know what's fantasy. But it's not really funny. I'm funny. I'm serious. You should like me. *Simon.* That wasn't funny. I'm funny though. Serious. I am. Fuuzzz. *(Short, nervous laugh.)* Shoot.

I've been shot. I shot someone. You don't

forget. I've been shot. I have one lung. Bullet just missed my heart, lodged itself in the back of my lung. I have no left lung, and I went back to crack after cleaning up my thug life, because that's what addiction does—turns your spine into a snake and you slither. Instead of stand. Naah. What do you want me to say? I'm clean in here. Prison. Nothing to steal but time. It's like watching a play.

A MOTHER IS COACHING HER SON
IN BASEBALL BUT AT THE SAME TIME

JOSÉ

Okay, Papo, yu reddy? I want yu to concentrate. I want yu to tsink homeron. Bend yu knees, bend yu knees. Keep yu hands together. Okay. (*Throws the ball.*) Pero Papo, if yu don't bend yu knees, yu no gonna hit the ball. Now go gettit.

Déjame ver si los Jankees están

by Caridad de la Luz

INSTILLS IN HIM THE IMPORTANCE OF BEING RESPECTFUL TOWARD FAMILY

ganando. (*Puts on radio headset.*) Okay, dame la bola. (*Catches the ball.*) Qué, what? What did Abuelo tell yu? Primero practice and theng I take yu to MacDonalls. Wheng I say concentrate, no en Happy Meals, es en el basebol. Mira, pay attention. Ven a_a. Here.

Wheng I say concentrate, yu tsink about cheezberrgers. That's no good. Yu pay attention like en eschool, porque si no, Abuelo's no gonna buy yu the nice clothes like Abuelo wears. What yu mean? Que no soy yiggy, I'm yiggy. A que te meto en el yiggy.

Mira y también, no more coming home, right away MTV, MTV, MTV. Yu show respect and say, "Bendición Abuelo. Bendición Abuela." And what I say to yu? "Que Dios te bendiga y que la Virgen te favoresque y que te acompañe." What yu mean why? Because so God will bless yu.

THE EVIL EYE

by Raquel Valle Senties

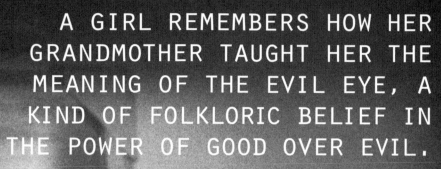

A GIRL REMEMBERS HOW HER GRANDMOTHER TAUGHT HER THE MEANING OF THE EVIL EYE, A KIND OF FOLKLORIC BELIEF IN THE POWER OF GOOD OVER EVIL.

My grandmother, Mamá Mine, loves to sit on her rocker on the front porch and watch the cars go by on San Barnardo Ave. On Saturdays, when I go spend the day with her, she tells me stories about the old days.

That was before, you know, before her dark, curly hair turned white and her green eyes needed glasses to see well. She knows everything. One day she asked me if I'd ever heard of the evil eye. When I said no, she answered that it was time I learned to protect myself against it. Mamá Mine says that if somebody looks at you because they think you're pretty, they have to touch you to hold off the evil eye or else you get sick and maybe even die. If they like the ring you're wearing, they better touch it or else you'll lose it or break it. She says that on the ranch where she grew up, the people tied red ribbons around the necks of their nicest animals to protect them from the evil eye. When my aunt Eunice got a fever, Mamá Mine decided someone had given her the evil eye. So she put an egg under my aunt's bed and left it there all night. In the morning she rubbed it all over my aunt's body. The evil eye went into the egg and my aunt Eunice was cured. My grandmother carefully broke the egg into a plate. It was shaped like an eye. I swear; I saw it!

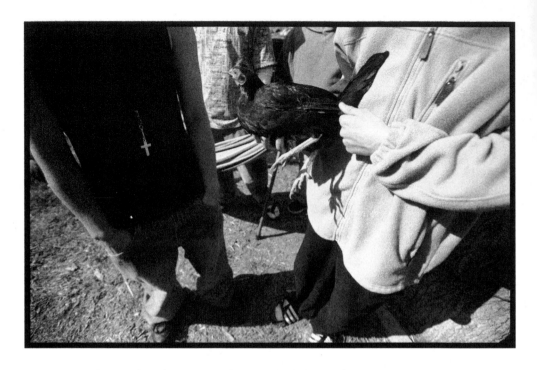

A BOY DESCRIBES EATING
HIS FAVORITE FOOD.

My mother raised me to think I was mainly a chicken eater. Being a Cuban lady, she cooked up dishes like *arroz con pollo*, *pollo asado*, and *sopa de pollo*. Each time I had chicken, I went crazy, maybe once or twice a week. We had chicken all the time, mainly because my father worked in a place where he could buy the chickens cheap. We had chicken sandwiches,

POULTRY

by Oscar Hijuelos, with respects to F. Kafka

chicken soups, fried chicken, chicken all the way.

As much as I liked the way chickens tasted, I owed my life to one of them. When I was about ten years old, I had gone upstate to a campground, and as we were sitting around eating some chicken, a great big nasty bear with giant teeth came out of the woods growling at us. Everybody ran away, but as the bear came after us, wanting to eat us humans, I threw a chicken leg at him. This big bear, nasty as he was, ate it, calmed down, and looked happy. (Quiz: True or false?) Anyway, I got home safe, but when I arrived at the door, all I wanted to do was eat more chicken.

Whenever any of my relatives or neighbors offered me a *piece of chicken*, I went crazy. I ate every kind of chicken: Cuban, Peruvian, Mexican chicken with mole. I ate so much chicken that one night I had this weird dream. I was thinking about all the chicken places in the neighborhood: Every shop had juicy rotisserie chickens in the window, and I *wanted* to eat them *all*. As it was a good dream, I ate maybe ten or fifteen deliciously roasted chickens in one day (true or false?). But even then I remembered each one of them with their crispy, honey-brown-colored skins. "*Qué sabroso!*" I said over and over again. You could not offer me a chicken dish—*pollo asado, pollo en fricasé, pollo* whatever—that I did not like.

MORPHOSIS

But then I went to sleep one night. My mother used to warn me about eating too much chicken: "*Hijo*," she said. "*Si comes tanto pollo, te conviertes en un pollo*," which is to say, "If you eat too much chicken, you will turn into one." But as I never believed her, I went to sleep one night and woke up in the morning with feathers; I do not know if I was a chicken, but I was still hungry for one.

LAST WEEK I WANTED

A GIRL, PLAGUED BY THOUGHTS OF NOT

by Susan Guevara

TO DIE

FITTING IN, CONTEMPLATES THE MEANING OF DEATH.

Last week I wanted to die. Not as in, "I was totally humiliated." Not because I say stupid things and never get what other people are talking about and am a lousy guitar player and don't fit in anyplace. Not a stoner, not a jock, not a goth, not a freak, not a geek, not a rah-rah, not a nada. Not even a real *chola*. No. I do not mean "die" as in the metaphor "I wanted to die from embarrassment."

I mean I *really* wanted to die. Like Steven Tanner from my seventh-grade homeroom class did, swinging by his skinny neck from his parents' garage ceiling. The real thing. But when I told the only person I knew well enough to tell, she said, "That's Satan talking! Don't *ever* talk like that again." Wow. My mother is such an authority on everything. Could she be right about this? Can Satan really talk through a person? If Satan can talk, then why not God? Does it take some special kind of person to get God speaking through you? That's it. I'm not good enough for God's voice. But Satan, well, Satan is doable. After all, he was that guy that fell to Earth. More my style.

All right then, if it's Satan talking, I'd like him to tell that stupid Mr. Hardesty that *Jonathan Livingston Seagull* is the dumbest book ever written. If he needs a talking bird to tell him how to be real, then he should sit in a tree and shit for a living. Instead of teaching bonehead English to somebody who at least knows that following some pack— or flock—isn't going to just happen. I mean, you don't just automatically fit in, you know.

Not to mention that ignorant Joe Rodriguez, who thinks my own original folk art birds look like so much "crap from Mexico." Not to mention Satan could say a thing or two to that dope of an art teacher, Joe Rodriguez, who probably has grandparents from Mexico just like me. Garbage can, trash can, Mexican. They laughed and laughed in that so very hip class of Joe Rodriguez's.

Now that I think on it, maybe Satan can act through me as well as talk. O Satan, rain down hell in tiny flaming pieces of sky on those jerks that hung Jason from a tree. Naked, tagged in black marker on his ass, his so-called girlfriend saying she knows nothing. Like she didn't see the sack on his head, the gun to his head, the gigantic, fat *pow* ringing through the pasture. Burn them up and keep them living, O Satan, I beg you.

Then, when I die, I will fly away with colored string and glass beads pasted to my wings. I will fly straight up to heaven, and I will take Satan with me. And if God doesn't like it, well, I'll just refuse to leave. Satan will have to let *me* do all of the talking this time. I can't really see myself convincing God of anything, but we could at least have a conversation. Maybe He'd be interested in my poetry. Maybe He'd let me speak in the language of my father and my grandfather. Maybe then He'd see my dying wasn't such a bad idea. Satan and I could keep Him company. And I bet the sunsets wouldn't hurt so much from up there.

Last week I wanted to die. And you know what? Nothing much has changed.

by Trinidad Sánchez Jr.

A BOY IS TELLING HIS SOCIAL WORKER ABOUT HIS ABUSIVE FATHER.

"Last night when I got home, Daddy was stupid drunk and he whipped me . . . started yelling and beat the crap out of me! Daddy whipped me into submission, whipped me into being the good son. . . . I don't understand how Daddy beats his own kin. I'm mad at my father, I'm mad at my father. . . ." Heard my words covering the wounds, and

I'M MAD AT

suspending any guilt on the part of Daddy, I continued, "I needed to be whipped; it was my fault!" It's in the quiet that the screams come to me . . . in the dark I hear them loud and clear. I can't sleep. I reached behind, took the end of my T-shirt, and pulled it up over my head, turning my back, revealing the welt marks stretched across it, and saw the disbelief on the face of the social worker, as he hadn't understood until then why I'd be mad at my father. . . .

MY FATHER

A RECENT TEENAGE IMMIGRANT MEDITATES ON WHAT SHE MISSES ABOUT HER HOMELAND.

TRANSLATING

At night my memory is sharp. . . . In the darkness of my room I translate the things of light. I observe certain rituals. The first is imagining the stars of my country. I name them out loud: the Three Marias, the Southern Cross, and of course Venus, which always accompanies me. She is my guardian angel, the lantern of dawn. After naming the stars, I caress the spines of my books. I've traveled with them, and they keep me company here so far away from home, in my loneliness. I like to have them close, I touch and open them, always, before I go to sleep. The language that I left behind calms me in blue. My last ritual is looking at my two shoes of different colors. My blue shoe calls me to the sea, that hoarse and booming sea that covered my face and my dreams. The other shoe is black, making me remember the winter of my new life here, the too-early darkness. Each

by Marjorie Agosín

of these shoes waits at the shore of my feet, reminding me
of who I was and who I am. Always by my side, showing me
the way. At night my memory is sharp, and I dream clearly.

THINGS

ON WHAT COULD PUSH SOMEONE INTO DOING

MURDER

by Michael Mejias

THE UNTHINKABLE:

!EGO!

(Alejandro Perez Perez, Latino, sixteen, is in custody for setting a
South Bronx social club on fire, killing thirty-three people. Presently
he is being interviewed by homicide detectives.)

I guess I'm in here because those bitches out there were still wanting to call me Parkay and shit. . . .

(*Silence.*)

Parkay, m-f's, like the butter.

They call me Parkay; even though I tell them it ain't *EVEN* like that and they trippin'. But m-f's don't listen, and that's why shit went down the way it did, yo.

I guess you gonna try to infiltrate the recess of my mind to find out why I killed all them peoples.

I'll tell you all the same shit I tell them bitch cops when they brung me in this shit jail. My heart is a bucket full of hate, yo, and if you come up close on me, I'll dump it all over your stupid ass. You get all up in my shit, you gonna wind up with a head full of my hate, no lie.

My name is Alejandro Perez Perez. It used to be Alejandro Perez de Perez, but we lost the "de" somewhere along the way. Now it's just Perez Perez, but I go by Al P to the P. . . .

Unless m-f's wanna disrespect and call me Parkay. . . .

(*Silence.*)

Like the butter!

These mofos started all this Parkay shit because of my big bro, Ray-Ray. . . .

Ray-Ray Perez Perez.

They used to call him Fly Guy around the way because he had a way with the ladies—*la chica-chicas*, yo, no lie.

They used to say that he spent more time inside a woman than out. They used to say that you best watch your lady if Fly Guy was around. He slept with Denise Figueroa on the night she got married to David Colon. And he slept with Brenda Fernandez when she was pregnant with Tito's kid. Homebro was all kinds of a crazy gash hound.

Then one time at the club my

brother Ray-Ray Perez Perez, aka Fly Guy, got with this crazy good-looking bitch, yo. She was bowling-ball black with light eyes and a butt so big it could choke a goat, kid, no lie. And she was soying my big bro too, sweatin' his ass like he was in gym class.

Only thing was she was up under the arm of Big Carlo from Vyse Ave., yo.

(*Silence.*)

Yeah, that Big Carlo, bitches. What you think? M-f's killed more people than famine and shit.

But Fly Guy ain't even sweatin'

the situation 'cause he knows he got it like that, know what I'm sayin'?

So he goes up to her all bold like when she about to go pee. And he's all like, "What's up, Chocolate?"

She be smiling and laughing, and after a while they drop out into the shadows and shit.

Later this sister come back to Big Carlo all f-drunk.

Big Carlo don't say shit but to send her home.

Big Carlo's boys are known as the Ballbusters, and they drag Fly Guy out of the club to answer for what he did.

At first it was going to be a straight-out stomp down. But then one of them Ballbusters threw Fly Guy into all this wire that was just laying around, and it tore up his pants and shit. The next thing you know, they has it in they mind to get some booty off him.

And they do.

About six of them.
People watching.

When I got home from hanging on the Deuce, it was about one o'clock. People couldn't wait to tell me about what happened.

That's when they started calling out that my bro got "spread out."

"Yo, your brother is butter and that makes you Parkay. They gonna spread you like Parkay, Al P!"

Then they all start chanting "Parkay."

I got down there, and the lot by the club was empty but for one of them supermarket shopping carts. Only it didn't have any wheels.

Fly Guy was stuffed in the cart.

I dragged my big bro seventeen blocks.

We live on the first floor, so I brought him through the window. I didn't want his *abuelita* to see him like that.

After I put him in bed I got me

some gasoline from a construction
site I know about and went back to
the club.

    I went into the abandoned
building next to the club to avoid the
bouncers.

    I gasolined the entire wall
the building shares with the club.

    And I torched the m-f.

by Walkiris Portes

A TEEN MOTHER RECOUNTS THE DAY

HER CHILD WAS BORN.

Each thing I did then I did for the first time. Hearing my baby's heart made me happy. Knowing I was going to bring a new part of me into the world made me scared. I had on two blue nightgowns, with something wrapped around my stomach with a medical machine. My feet cold as ice. Hearing a lot of people whispering around me. Feeling this angry pain, urgent to come out. Changing rooms, hearing the screeching of the wheels, feeling the needle inside my vein, filling me with IVs. Seeing the strong light in my face. Couldn't take the pain no more, so I rang the nurse's bell so I could get the epidural. While the nurse came, I was pulling out my hair, screaming, and once I dropped a tear out of my eyes. I had my eyes closed very tight and was breathing very deep while I got the epidural. Seeing the green curtain gave me strength, faith. After the epidural I went to sleep and woke up at 7:00 a.m. I was feeling pressure like I had to go to the bathroom. Blood coming out of my vagina like crazy, feeling my heart as fast as Speedy Gonzales. I was angry seeing my boyfriend sleeping. But I realize he didn't want to see me suffer. Finally the time came. My boyfriend held one of my legs, and the nurse the other, then I push and push—there he was.

ME AMERICAN

WRITTEN IN RESPONSE TO THE MANNER IN
TREATED JESSE EACH TIME HE RETURNED
HOMETOWN, DETROIT, MICHIGAN.

Me American. I like to live in Amerri-ca. El Norte. Oye como vá.
English is the official language. Green Card. No Way José. Gringo.
Hispanic. Vaya con Diós. Boycott Grapes. Badges, we don't need no
stinking badges. Viva la Raza. Hey Cisco, Hey Pancho. Low Rider.
Taco Bell. Spic 'n' Span. Mojados. El Bárrio. Sal Si Puedes. Speedy
Gonzales. Salsa. Brown Power. Campesinos. La Bamba. Beaner. Hijo.
Macho. Mija. Malinche. P.R. Menudo. Cholos. Velvet paintings. Tico.
Desilu. Olé. Cuba libre. Latino. Zapata. Frito Bandito. Lambada.
Loyal consumers. Adiós. Spanish eyes. Chicana. Ranchera. Tejano.
Pizzarro. Incas. Corridos. Ganas. Che. Grito. Gaucho. Bolero. Rodeo.
Pan dulce. La familia. Cantinflas. INS. La Migra. Posada. Cha cha
cha. Cinco de Mayo. Minority. Diversity. LU LAC. Tex-Mex. Chili.
Zoot Suit. Jalapeño. Día de los Muertos. Unidos en la lucha. Piñatas.
Rio Grande. Tamales. Llama. Bilingual. La buena vida. Velveeta. La
cucaracha. Baseball has been very, very good to me. Conquistadores.
Mulatos. Estas son las mañanitas. El día de la Revolución. Un abrazo.

by Jesse Villegas

Mestizo. Amor. Sabor. Consafos. Nosotros 38 (?) million y más!
Multi-culture. ESL. Fiesta. ESPN. Free trade. Chiquita Banana.
Independista. Diós mío. Indio. Pueblo. Rivera. Kahlo. Paz.
Tradiciones. English spoken here. Me American, me here. Me
immigrant in my own land. Me American.

WHICH IMMIGRATION OFFICIALS
FROM WINDSOR, CANADA, TO HIS

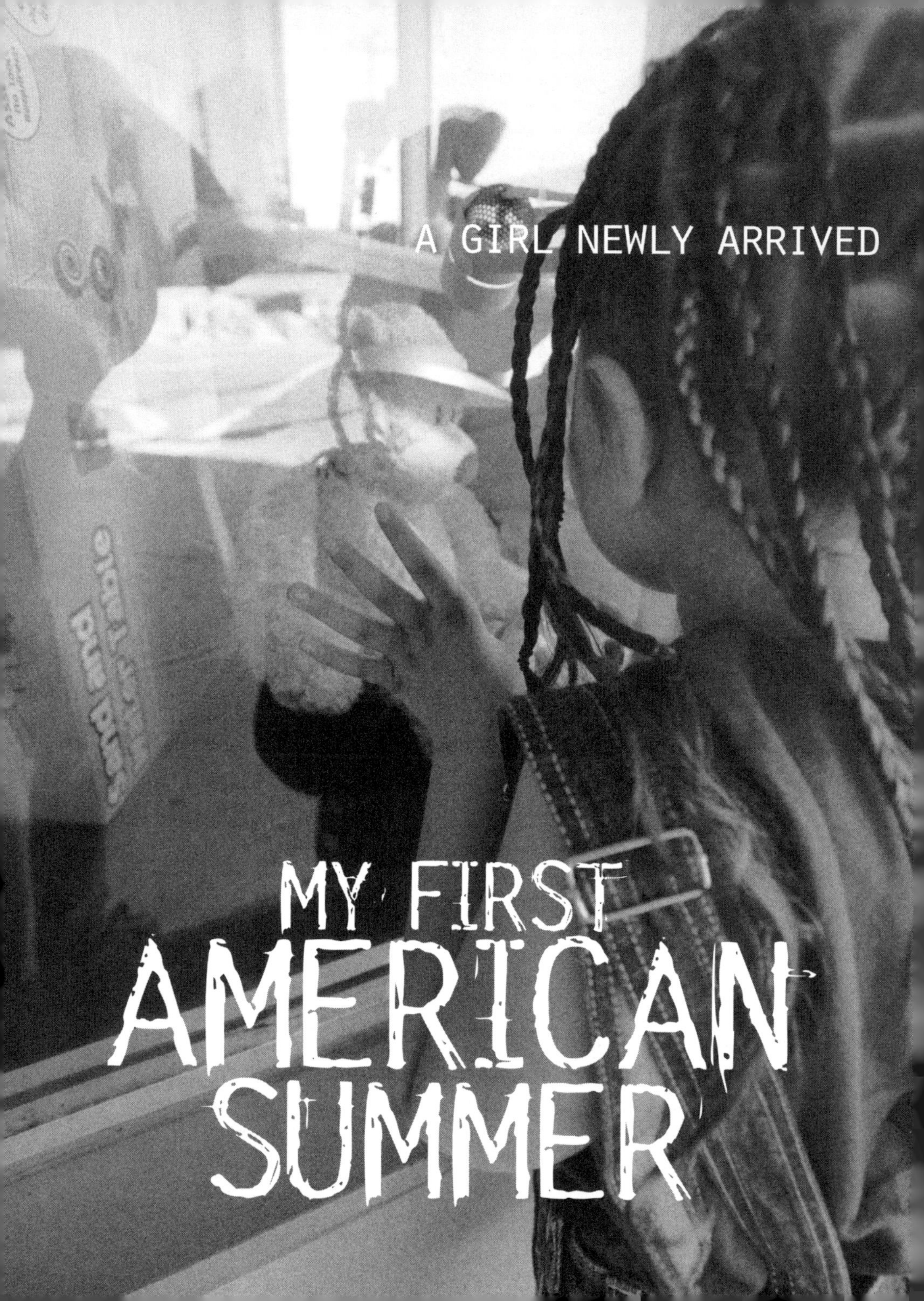

A GIRL NEWLY ARRIVED

MY FIRST
AMERICAN
SUMMER

by Lissette Mendez

FROM CUBA REMEMBERS DETAILS OF
HER FIRST AMERICAN SUMMER.

My first weeks in Miami are like bright photographs my memory shuffles with the dexterity of a Las Vegas cardsharp: My uncle and I crossing Washington Avenue at Lincoln Road, when I see, behind plate glass, the most beautiful dolls in the world—round eyes with lids that open and close, shiny, fat caramel curls—miniature Scarlett O'Haras in peach and aqua ruffled taffeta. At the pharmacy, fuzz-ball fridge magnets with rattling plastic eyes, felt feet glued to their undersides. These fuzzy magnets are hot pink and red, or yellow as the chicks I saw hatch just months before in the packed-dirt backyard of my friend's house in Havana. At Pantry Pride supermarket, the dog toys: squeezy burgers and pork chops and hot dogs. *I could really play house with these*, I think. And the candy racks by the registers. Once, because I have no coins of my own and am too embarrassed to ask the grandmother I just met, I steal a pack of Cinn-A-Burst. White sunshine, like knives slicing through the windows, makes brilliant the red Kit Kat bars, cream yellow Whatchamacallits, and slick-white, bumpy Almond Joys as I slip the gum in my pocket and walk out the mechanical door.

43

A GIRL DESCRIBES HER

GOD SMELLS LIKE A ROAST PIG

from Midnight Sandwich/Medianoche

by Melinda Lopez

FAMILY TRADITION OF MAKING *LECHÓN*, OR ROAST PORK, A FAVORITE DISH.

Do you know what's really good? You take a pig, gut it, wash it inside and out, and then you get about six or seven *tías*. Two are peeling and mashing garlic, and one is making small cuts all over the pig, and putting garlic in each little cut. One *tía* is taking olive oil by the hand full and rubbing all over the pig and another is doing the same with lemons.

Here comes another *tía* with a big jug of wine and
pouring some into everyone's mouth, so that they
don't have to stop working. And the women are all
laughing and shouting for their husbands to make
sure the kids haven't drowned in the pool. Now, the
husbands are taking advantage of the fact that the
women have all busy hands to rub up against them
and cop a feel, *Ay, cabrón! Déjame en paz!* or maybe,
if everyone is drunk enough, to get a really good
kiss out of it. And the grandmother is sitting in the
chair, crocheting bikinis, saying more olive oil, more
garlic, did you do the ears? Don't forget the ears,
no I didn't forget the ears, but they don't look done,
they are, the ears have been oiled and lemoned, and
salted, and are happily marinating, this joyful pig.

And you let it soak for about twenty hours.

And then about two o'clock in the morning,
someone starts screaming, *el puerco el puerco se
escapó*—the pig is escaping, the pig is getting away,
and lights go on all over the house, as couples
stumble out to see what happened. Was it a dog was
it a fox? And the men wish they had their guns. And

then someone's calling the pool the pool, and we all run out to the pool . . .

. . . and there's the pig. Floating on a raft in the middle of the water. Wearing sunglasses. Ay ay ay the party-party has begun—And the next day, the men start the fire, and someone loses an eyebrow. And then they come like a procession with that glorious oiled and marinated pig, and splay him across the bed of chicken wire. And that dear, tender, and some say highly intelligent animal (smarter than a dog some say) cooks in the yard all day. And the smell is like . . . that's what God smells like. God smells like a roast pig on a summer's day.

OH, BEAUTIFUL?

THE SON OF TWO CUBAN EXILES EXPERIENCES THE UGLINESS

I was born in the United States, the son of two Cuban exiles who reluctantly abandoned their homeland, exiles from an oppressive dictator and the disillusionment of the false emancipator and traitor to the principles of freedom and justice that followed. They were young idealists seeking a refuge, an oasis from the mendacity and corruption that have plagued Cuba for centuries. Like all of America's orphaned children, they came upon her promising shores with faith and hope in the higher moral ground and opportunity they held.

I was a child of the sixties. My father always sang the praises of our adoptive country and every day gave thanks in prayer at our dinner table to have his family safe and sound in the greatest country in the world, a country of freedom, principles, morality, a country where a decent, honest man could accomplish literally anything. At home we spoke Spanish, but once out the door, I was forbidden to speak anything but English.

In 1969, when the Apollo astronauts landed on the moon, he shook me awake in tears and said, "Look, René, see, here anything is possible." In my starry-eyed, eight-year-old, somnambulant state, I stared, incredulous at the black-and-white images, in awe and admiration as Neil Armstrong heralded one giant leap for mankind. The moment is etched in my mind as surely as a diamond engraves a stone. For my tender years I well understood the majesty of the

by René Pedraza del Prado

OF PREJUDICE IN AMERICA.

moment. For months afterward I drew endless sketches of rocket ships, planets, stars. I would sway upon a swing in our backyard at twilight and, looking up at heaven, revealing her jewels one by one, sing "God Bless America" over and over, in such pride and true love for my country; to this day it is my favorite patriotic hymn. One day I, too, would reach them. Some way I, too, would touch the sky.

Back at school in my third-grade classroom, when my teacher asked the assembled children what we aspired to become when we grew up, I responded self-assuredly, still imbued with my astral passion, "An astronaut or an actor or a magician!" She looked back at me with barely veiled derision and scornfully replied,

"I'm so sorry to hear that, René, because your people, Cuban people, are marked to be janitors or garbage collectors." Another time, when I was distractedly singing a song to myself in class, lost in my childhood reveries, she marched to my desk and asked that I put my hands out before me. Trusting her (for I loved her in spite of herself), I did just that; she then violently struck a ruler across my knuckles and said, "Next time you'll learn to be quiet in class and begin to become a good citizen." I walked home alone, crying the distance, feeling, feeling. I have never forgotten, forgiven.

This was my first bitter taste of the humiliation and degradation that is too often the foul fruit of prejudice and ignorance, a fruit I would come to taste too often in our beloved America the Beautiful, America the Free, America the Equal, with liberty, justice for all.

My father also learned this rancid truth, and yet he never lost his childlike passion and admiration for the people of this great country, even as he discovered that he was not destined as one of these great and powerful titans. He erroneously felt that it was he who had fallen short of the mark, he who was lacking and found wanting. He kept us in good middle-class comforts, and even luxuries, but little by little his sense of self and identity was chiseled and fragmented and crumbled in small but irrevocable ways; such is the fate of the exile, transplanted from his

natural state, domain, province. As I grew up, I witnessed this once proud and genially charming man begin to bend his shoulders, saw his dazzling smile become progressively a sad and lamentable frown.

I am glad he died before the rot of this fruit, like a metastasized cancer, spread like a wildfire of greed and corruption, distortion and degradation, that has made our modern-day nation unrecognizable from the leading force of human rights and dignity it once had the moral right to impeach the entire world with.

Had he lived long enough, he might have realized that, but for the glories of material abundance, his cherished beacon had dimmed to a dull and feeble shadow of its past and true greatness and had begun to look more and more like the same beast he'd fled from all those years ago.

Could he have borne the criminal, vulgar, and terrifying decimation of all he dearly held to be the highest of human values, the decent tenets of a civilized world now run afoul by a thirst for power and conquest at any price over the eternal verities of morality and common decency?

I think not; but it doesn't matter anyway, for he died of a broken heart just in time, before this unyielding, unrelenting monster reared its ugly head: unabashed, unashamed, unrepentant, unmoved, unprincipled, and un-American.

As for my heart, it beats on, fighting against all the terrible evidence, hoping to leave a mark, a glimmer of hope, of beauty, of love . . . for the sake of all those little unborn astronauts, actors, and magicians of the world to come, that they might perhaps have something of better value to hold in their future hands besides a mere dollar bill to reckon their self-worth with. I yet still love my country.

FUTUREBOY

A BOY WONDERS ABOUT THE
ESSENCE OF HIS VOICE.

I don't know where
My voice comes from.

A tree?
Sometimes I can feel its branches,
Sharp, broken, thin as a leaf, so thin
My mother peeks through its rain-colored skin,
So skinny you can barely hear it sway and play.

Does my voice come from the sea?
Sometimes the wild wave roars out
And I go about tossing and splashing
Into chairs and open doors in class
And I sigh, "Where, where?"

Then
My voice floats up and away,
Sits quietly, alone
On a cloud—tomorrow it echoes
Across a blue mountain,
Today, today, it whispers

by Juan Felipe Herrera

When it whisps back to me.

Or maybe it comes from me,
Only me.

And the ocean
And the cloud
And the tree.

by Elaine Romero

EMILY, AN
EIGHTEEN-
YEAR-OLD GIRL
DRESSED IN
JEANS, SITS
IN A CAFÉ.

EMILY

We've been sitting here in this crowded café. I can't tell you if it's been five minutes or an hour. We started right into it. Like we could trust each other. You've already convinced me that you're my clone, except you have a . . . you know. You've been creeping next to me ever so slowly. Don't think I haven't noticed. Our thighs are unofficially touching. (*Beat.*) You lift your hand. It hangs in the air. In suspended animation. Waiting to touch my knee. (*Beat.*)

You stop. Your hand drops. In your eyes I see your reluctance. It gives you away. Past failures. Heartbreaks hanging in the closet. You look me in the eye. Real precise. We swap souls for a second. You feel my fear. So, you feel better now. More relaxed. You move even closer. Our thighs are undeniably touching. (*Beat.*) And you're making me laugh. I see a snapshot of us. Both in jeans. Thinking the same thoughts, feeling the same feelings. Why is it you won't put your hand on my knee? (*Short beat.*) Ah, that's nice. I should've thought of that myself. You're playing with the hairs on my forearm. A delightful idea. Oh, no. You're turning your hand over. Stroking my arm with the back of your hand. You catch my panic. You stop. I can breathe again. Back to the thigh. Good idea. Oh, no. You're dangerously close to the hole in my jeans. You found it. Of course you did. The hole's there for everybody to see. Strung together by a few threads in my jeans. Oh, no. You're moving your fingers. I must tell you. You have beautiful, very intelligent fingers. Oh, God. They broke a thread. I refuse to look. I refuse to feel your hand on my knee. On my skin. Oh, don't do that. Don't lift your fingers up like that. I don't even know you.

(*Beat.*) Why'd you stop? You withdrew your hand from the hole in my jeans. You patted the loose threads with your hand. Oh, no, don't go. Let's go back. To the innocence. Skin protected by lots of material. Then slowly, ever so slowly, start to move toward me, thigh pressing against thigh. And I'll start to feel you breathe, and I'll feel myself breathe. In sync with you. And we'll talk. Simply at first. And then we'll tell more. We'll tell everything, you and me. And then, maybe, I'll let you wander back to the hole in my jeans.

by Elaine Romero

(*Dreamily*) I saw her. She spoke to me, the Snowcap Queen. She came to me like a vision—blue and blue, standing on a tub of lard. And you were all there. Amy and Mami. Sorry, Abuelo, you weren't there, but the rest of you were. She came to me and she said, "I am from the Andes. I am your Indian mother—no, I am your mestiza mother. I know the ways of our people, and we have always swum in rivers of fat and felt those little fat cells pulsating

SYLVIA, WHO IS PASSED OUT ON HER *ABUELO*'S LAWN MOWER, COMES TO CONSCIOUSNESS.

SYLVIA

through our veins so we could feel alive again. That is our history. That is our *destino*," she says. "That is the real *dieta de la raza, mi'ja*." (*Beat.*) And she said no more lettuce for a while. Yuck. (*Sylvia spits.*) No more of that vile green leafy stuff until I bleed.

by Quiara Alegría Hudes

BARRIO ABCs

(*Two kids from the barrio are competing
for the most original description of their
hometown. their voices and energy tell the
story of a neighborhood. it's like they look
through binoculars and see city blocks as
they speak. it's like they peek into hundreds
of windows in the barrio, and each time
they see a different world, snooping into
people's lives through little keyholes.*)

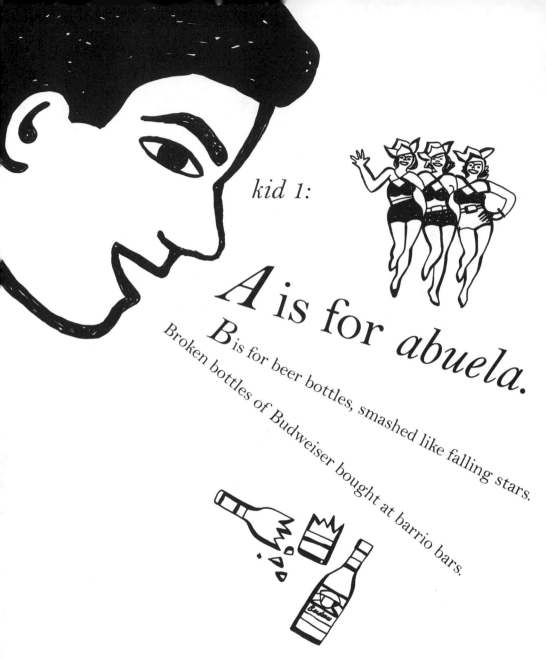

kid 1:

A is for abuela.

B is for beer bottles, smashed like falling stars.

Broken bottles of Budweiser bought at barrio bars.

kid 2:

And abandoned car.

C is for collecting cans for cash,

cents
recycled at Seventh
and Girard.

kid 1: **D** is for dominoes. Abuela taught me to play.
Double six dominoes during summer days.

kid 2: **E** is for the echo of the elevated train.

kid 1: **F** is for the fire hydrants spraying summer rain.

kid 2: **F** is for my family's favorite Philadelphia fountains.
Eakins Oval, LoganCircle, like the
waterfalling foam of El Yunque's
far-off mountains.

kid 1: **G** is for graffiti.

kid 2: And for gentrification.

kid 1: **H** is for the have-nots. Holding out their humble hands
and empty cans in hopes of a donation.

kid 2: I is for the ice cream truck in infinite flavors so sweet.

kid 1: J is for *los jíbaros* jamming in the jungle of concrete.

kid 2: K is for kaleidoscopic kin.
For Spanish blood, for African blood, for Arawak, Taino, Chino,
mixing in our skin.

kid 1: L is for the ladies who lounge at living-room ledges
and look at life go by.
But never let life in.

kid 2: M is for machete, how my ancestors carved their fields.

kid 1: Now I use a microwave to cultivate my meals.

kid 2: M is for *muralistas,* making murals of island vistas.
Using acrylic medium to brighten the brick wall tedium.

kid 1: N is for the next-door neighbor who nurses my grandma
when she has asthma.

.

kid 2: O is for Ontario and oh so many other
one-way streets within the barrio.

kid 1: P is for propaganda. For playing pots and pans.
For the Puerto Rican Day Parade and proudly singing as loud as you can.

kid 2: Q is for *quiosco,* for kiosks serving beer. *Tostones, maduros,*
the *Daily News, bacalaitos,* and deep-fried cheer.

kid 1: Q is for *quemar,* to burn a house to the ground beneath,
making a block full of row homes look like a smile that's missing
its two front teeth.

kid 2: For rituals at the riverbank, for roosters and roaring rrrrrahdio,
a rolling R remains forever rooted in the barrio.

kid 1: # Remember.

kid 2: For rice and beans and recipes that help us know our history.
One pack *sazón*, homemade *sofrito*, potato, tomato sauce, *ay bendito.*

kid 1: # Remember.

kid 2: Vienna sausages. Spanish olives. Fresh cilantro. *Calabaza.*

kid 1: *S* is for the Spanish I speak in silent prayers and slippery rhymes.
S is for the syllabic systems of Spanish and English in syncopated time.
S is the language my grandfather knew of,
S is the language I'll never be sure of.
S is the sensual stories sprouting from soil in San Juan and Santurce,
stowed away in the sidewalk and stucco of North Philadelphia today.
S is the slangy Spanglish swaying on northbound subway cars.
S is the salsa songs of salty summers and island stars.
The *S* I know is slipping away, silence falls on my tongue.
I strive to keep the *S* in my mouth, I work to keep the *S* in my fist,
for *S* is the story that says where I come from.

kid 2: T is for time.

kid 1: U is for under. Underground. Underneath.

kid 2: V is for the verdant vegetable plot reinventing a vanquished empty lot.

kid 1: W is for wise.

kid 2: X is for XXXL, your favorite T-shirt size.

kid 1: Y is for youthfully yelling as loud as you can and for a smile that looks as big as a yucca or a yam.

kid 2: Z is for zone. Empowerment zone. Drug-free zone. No-parking zone. Construction zone.

kid 1: For zilch. What some may see as zero, this alphabetic barrio,

where stories zoom by every block you go,

this is my home.

by Sandra Cisneros

A GIRL RECOUNTS HER FRIEND'S
DEFINITION OF GOD.

DARIUS AND

You can never have too much sky. You can fall asleep and wake up drunk on sky, and sky can keep you safe when you are sad. Here there is too much sadness and not enough sky. Butterflies, too, are few and so are flowers and most things that are beautiful. Still, we take what we can get and make the best of it.

Darius, who doesn't like school, who is sometimes stupid and mostly a fool, said something wise today, though most days he says nothing. Darius, who chases girls with firecrackers or a stick that touched a rat and thinks he's tough, today pointed up because the world was full of clouds, the kind like pillows.

"You all see that cloud, that fat one there?" Darius said. "See that?" "Where?" "That one next to the one that looks like popcorn. That one there. See that? That's God," Darius said. "God?" somebody little asked. "God," he said, and made it simple.

THE CLOUDS

BIOGRAPHICAL NOTES

Marjorie Agosín was born in Chile. She is currently a professor of Spanish at Wellesley College and has received many awards, including the United Nations Leadership Award in Human Rights. She has published more than twenty books of poetry, as well as eight memoirs and six books of fiction. Among her poetry volumes are *At the Threshold of Memory*, *Dear Anne Frank*, *Las Chicas Desobedientes*, and *Conchalí*.

Claudia Quiroz Cahill is a poet of Bolivian heritage. She holds an MFA in creative writing from Columbia University. Her work has appeared in *River Styx* and *Antaeus* as well as in the anthologies *Cool Salsa* and *Red Hot Salsa*. She lives in Virginia.

Gwylym Cano is a poet who lives in Denver, Colorado. He holds a James Ryan Morris Memorial Tombstone Award for Poetry. He also acts, having worked with El Centro Su Teatro, the Bilingual Foundation of the Arts, and Danza Floricanto/USA. Mr. Cano owns and operates an independent film company, Fool Moon Productions. He says he is "the world's only living Welsh-Xicano."

Sandra Cisneros, a Chicana, is one of America's best-known poets. Among her books of fiction and poetry are *Caramelo* and *My Wicked, Wicked Ways*. Her *House on Mango Street* has sold more than a million copies. She is the recipient of a MacArthur Fellowship and lives in San Antonio, Texas.

Susan Guevara was born and raised in the Bay Area of California. She received her BFA degree in illustration from the Academy of Art College in San Francisco and studied privately under the Flemish impressionist painter Remy Van Sluys, as well as attending the Royal Academy of Fine Art in Mechlin, Belgium. She has been illustrating picture books since 1989 and is the recipient of numerous awards, including the Tomás Rivera award. Her illustrative work for *Chato Goes Cruisin'*, by Gary Soto, was selected as one of the *New York Times* Best Illustrated Books of 2005. She lives in an old adobe in northern New Mexico.

Juan Felipe Herrera is of Mexican-American background and grew up in California. He has written poetry books for people of all ages, among them *Laughing Out Loud, I Fly.* His novels include *CrashBoomLove* and *Cinnamon Girl.* He is also an actor, a playwright, and a professor of Latin American studies in Fresno, where he lives with his family.

Oscar Hijuelos, a native New Yorker, is the son of Cuban immigrants and the first Latino to win the Pulitzer Prize in fiction, in 1990. He has written seven novels, among them *Our House in the Last World,* which won the Rome Prize in 1984; *The Mambo Kings Play Songs of Love; Mr. Ives' Christmas;* and, most recently, *Dark Dude,* to be released in fall of 2008.

Quiara Alegría Hudes holds an MFA in playwriting from Brown University and a BA in music composition from Yale. Her plays include *The Adventures of Barrio Grrrl!; Yemaya's Belly; Elliot, A Soldier's Fugue;* and *In the Heights,* a Broadway musical. She has been honored with a Clauder Prize, the Paula Vogel Award in Playwriting, and the Kennedy Center American College Theater Festival Latina Playwriting Award. She has been a resident playwright at New Dramatists.

Caridad de la Luz, aka La Bruja, is a Puerto Rican poet/multitalent born and raised in the Boogie Down Bronx. She has been heard from Switzerland to San Francisco, from Poland to Puerto Rico—check her Web site at www.labrujanyc.com. She continues to bless mics, stages, radio stations, music videos, and, most recently, the silver screen.

Melinda Lopez is a playwright and actress. The first recipient of the Charlotte Woolard Award, given by the Kennedy Center to a "promising new voice in American theatre," she has written many award-winning plays, including *Sonia Flew, God Smells Like a Roast Pig, Midnight Sandwich/Medianoche, How Do You Spell Hope?,* and *Scenes from a Bordello.* She teaches theater and performance at Wellesley College.

Michael Mejias was born and raised in the Bronx and was educated in Catholic schools and Hunter College/City University of New York. He's worked as a playwright, dramaturg, literary manager, director, monologue coach, professor, and producer. He is the founder and curator of the Reading Series at the Kettle of Fish (in Greenwich Village, NYC) and the Co-Executive Producer/Theatre Programming of the Loisaida Cortos Latino Film Festival. For the last ten years, Michael Mejias has worked at Writers House, a literary agency.

Lissette Mendez is a Cuban who came to the United States in the Mariel boat lift in 1980. A program coordinator at the Florida Center for the Literary Arts at Miami Dade College, she writes nonfiction and poetry. Her work has been published in anthologies and literary journals, including *Blue Mesa Review, TriQuarterly, Kalliope,* and *Rattle.*

Walkiris Portes is a graduate of Brandeis High School. Her essay titled "Birth" was first published in a booklet about teenage motherhood.

René Pedraza del Prado lives in Washington, DC, where he writes and gardens. He is the son of the renowned Cuban poet Pura del Prado, deceased. He is an actor by trade and writes by genetic impulse.

Elaine Romero's plays, which include *Barrio Hollywood, Secret Things, ¡Curanderas! Serpents of the Clouds,* and *Day of Our Dead,* have been presented by such groups as Actors Theatre of Louisville, the Arizona Theatre Company, Women's Project and Productions, San Diego Repertory Theatre, and INTAR. A past guest artist at South Coast Repertory, she has served as playwright in residence at the Arizona Theatre Company, managing their National Latino Playwrights Award.

Trinidad Sánchez Jr. was a nationally known and beloved Chicano poet and author who lectured extensively at schools, universities, and literary and cultural centers. Among his best-known books are *Why Am I So Brown?* and the chapbooks *Authentic Chicano Food Is Hot!* and *Poems by Father and Son.* He lived in San Antonio, Texas, at the time of his death in 2006.

Raquel Valle Sentíes is a poet, playwright, and painter from Texas. She is the manager of the bookstore El Café del Barrio in Laredo. Her book of poetry *Soy Como Soy y Qué* received Mexico's José Fuentes Mares national literature award in 1997.

Esmeralda Santiago is an acclaimed Puerto Rican memoirist whose work *When I Was Puerto Rican* is on recommended reading lists at high schools and universities throughout the country. She is an active member of the New York City literary community.

Michele Serros is an award-winning, frequently anthologized poet and commentator. The author of the poetry volume *Chicana Falsa* and the story collection *How to Be a Chicana Role Model,* she has taught poetry in inner-city schools and women's prisons through the PEN Center USA West's programs. She lives in New York City.

Gary Soto was born and raised in Fresno, California. He is a prolific writer of books of prose, poetry, and drama, including *Buried Onions, Living Up the Street, Baseball in April, Nerdlandia,* and *Local News.* He has written an opera and produced films for Spanish-speaking children. He is the editor of *Pieces of the Heart: New Chicano Fiction.*

Jesse Villegas lives in Detroit. He was born in Houston, Texas, and raised in "Bloody Fifthward." He arrived in Michigan, via Orlando, Florida. He is an artist, theater director, and actor. He considers himself *Amor y paz,* the "Last Latino Beat."

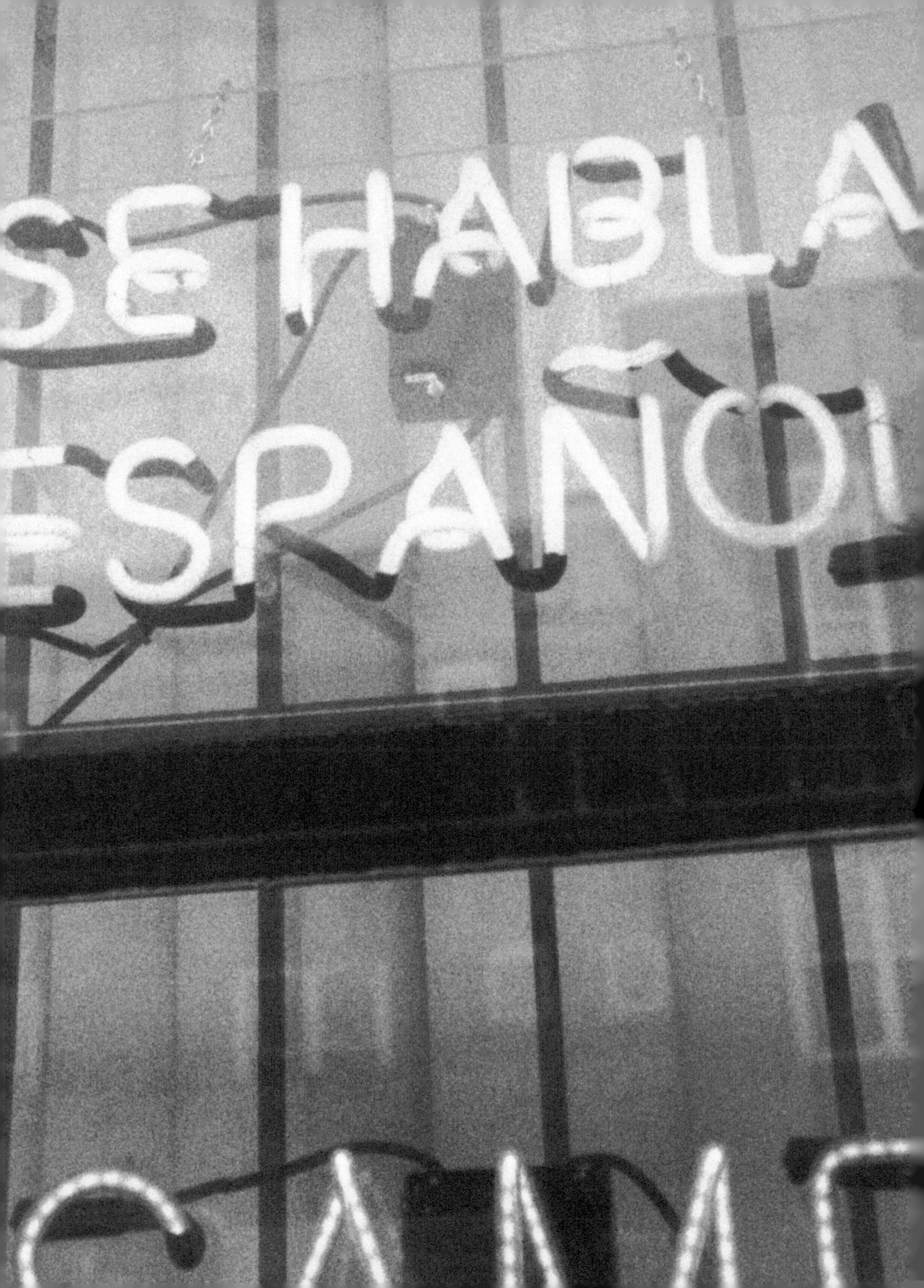
SE HABLA
SPAÑO

COPYRIGHT ACKNOWLEDGMENTS

Lori Marie Carlson was born in Jamestown, New York. After attending public schools she received her BA in Spanish literature and linguistics from the College of Wooster in Wooster, Ohio. She received her MA in Hispanic literature from Indiana University, Bloomington in 1981. After completing her studies she was deputy director, and then director, of literature at the Americas Society in New York City. She has taught in the Spanish departments of Indiana University, Columbia University and New York University. Currently she is a faculty member in the English department at Duke University. Among her books are the landmark, award-winning bilingual poetry collections *Cool Salsa* and *Red Hot Salsa*, as well as the novels *The Sunday Tertulia* and *The Flamboyant*. Among the awards her books have received are ALA Best Book for Young Adults, *School Library Journal* Book of the Year, *Horn Book*'s Fanfare, *The Bulletin*'s Blue Ribbon, the Americas Award Commended Title, and the White Ravens for International Distinction. She resides in New York City and Durham, North Carolina.

Manuel Rivera-Ortiz is a photographer who was born in Guayama, Puerto Rico. His documentary work depicts poverty and stories of hardship and hope throughout the third world. His photographs marry journalism and the very personal experience of his childhood growing up poor in outposts throughout southern Puerto Rico. In this compilation, Rivera-Ortiz deviates slightly from his distinctive photo reportage style. Instead of focusing on the very real lives of people living poor, he has captured a creative, illustrative imagery indicative of the very poignant stories told by the writers in this book. All subjects depicted in the images are Latino; all images were produced in Latino neighborhoods from NYC to Ohio.

His award-winning images have been exhibited internationally, and are a part of the permanent collections of the George Eastman House International Museum of Photography and Film, the Lehigh University Art Galleries, the William Whipple Art Gallery and Museum, Columbia University's Joseph Pulitzer Graduate School of Journalism. Rivera-Ortiz holds an MS in journalism from Columbia University in New York City.

Flavio Morais was born in São Paolo, Brazil, where he first worked as an illustrator for a T-shirt company. He then moved to London and attended an Art and Design course at Chelsea College of Art; and eventually moved to Barcelona, where he still lives and works on art for press, editorial, and advertising. Some of his works include TV animations, installations, and mural paintings done for clients such as: Once, *La Vanguardia*, *El Pais*, *El Mundo*, *Avui*, Saatchi & Saatchi, Thompson, Canal +, Spanish TV, Italian TV, Volkswagen, Coca-Cola (Texas), Café Ducados (Madrid), Sampaka (Valencia), Cocktail Bar Negroni, Restaurant Spin (Shanghai), and Ed.Abril (Brazil). Apart from the commissioned works, he also held several individual exhibitions in Spain, Brazil, and Paris.

He has a special love for the popular culture made in Africa, Bahia, and Mexico, and works done by people without any knowledge of Art—art-brut and outsiders. Music keeps him alive. . . . turn the music off and there will be no more Flavio Morais!